Dear Parent:

Your child's love of reading

Every child learns to read in a different way a
speed. Some go back and forth between reading levels and read
favorite books again and again. Others read through each level in
order. You can help your young reader improve and become more
confident by encouraging his or her own interests and abilities. From
books your child reads with you to the first books he or she reads
alone, there are I Can Read Books for every stage of reading:

SHARED READING
Basic language, word repetition, and whimsical illustrations,
ideal for sharing with your emergent reader

BEGINNING READING
Short sentences, familiar words, and simple concepts
for children eager to read on their own

READING WITH HELP
Engaging stories, longer sentences, and language play
for developing readers

READING ALONE
Complex plots, challenging vocabulary, and high-interest topics
for the independent reader

I Can Read Books have introduced children to the joy of reading
since 1957. Featuring award-winning authors and illustrators and a
fabulous cast of beloved characters, I Can Read Books set the
standard for beginning readers.

A lifetime of discovery begins with the magical words **"I Can Read!"**

Visit www.icanread.com for information
on enriching your child's reading experience.

*For my dad, who passed
on his love for origami to
me and patiently taught
me how to make all sorts
of wonderful creations
when I was Gigi's age.
—M.I.*

I Can Read® and I Can Read Book® are trademarks of HarperCollins Publishers.

Gigi and Ojiji: Perfect Paper Cranes

Library of Congress Control Number: 2023943332
ISBN 978-0-06-320815-5 (trade bdg.) — ISBN 978-0-06-320814-8 (pbk.)

24 25 26 27 28   COS   10 9 8 7 6 5 4 3 2 1   First Edition

GIGI AND OJIJI

PERFECT
PAPER CRANES

MELISSA IWAI

HARPER

An Imprint of HarperCollinsPublishers

Gigi loved the Japan Day Festival.
There was yummy food,
a parade, and craft booths!

This year, Gigi's grandfather Ojiji
was helping at the origami booth!
Origami is the art of paper folding.
"I want to make a crane!" said Gigi.

"A crane is hard," said Mom.

"Ganbatte!"

Gigi knew that meant good luck—

do your best!

"Ganbarimasu!" Gigi answered.

That means I will try my best!

But when Gigi got to the booth
there was a long line!

"Do you want to learn how to fold
a puppy?" a helper asked.
"Why don't you try while you wait,"
said Mom.

Gigi chose her origami paper.
The nice woman showed her
how to make a puppy.

"Ta-da!" said Gigi.

"I love origami!

I want to show Ojiji!"

Then Gigi saw the other kids' cranes.

Her puppy didn't seem very great.

Gigi crumpled her puppy into her pocket.

"I want to learn how to make a crane!"

said Gigi.

She joined the other kids Ojiji was teaching.

"Ganbatte!" said Mom.

"Ganbarimasu!" said Gigi.

Gigi tried to keep up with Ojiji
and the other kids.

"Folding a crane is hard!" said Gigi.

"It took me a while to learn how
when I was a kid," said Mom.

Gigi tried and tried.

It was much harder than the puppy.

"I can't do it," Gigi said.

"This is no fun.

I don't like origami."

"Ganbatte," Ojiji said.

"One fold at a time . . ."

"One fold at a time," thought Gigi.

"I can do that."

"Ganbarimasu!" she said.

At last, Gigi made a crane!

"You did it!" said Ojiji.

Ojiji set Gigi's crane next to his.

"Oh no!" said Gigi.

"What?" said Mom.

"My crane is so bad!"

Gigi burst into tears.

"Hey, what's going on?" asked Dad.

"I can't do origami!" said Gigi.

"It looks like you made a crane!" said Dad.

"But my crane isn't as good
as Ojiji's!" said Gigi.

"It's your very first crane!" said Mom.

"I'm so proud of you," said Ojiji.

"You stuck with it.

You didn't give up!"

"Remember one fold at a time?"
Ojiji asked.

Gigi nodded yes.

"Just make one crane at a time
and keep going."

Gigi felt better.

Someday maybe her cranes
would be as good as Ojiji's.

"Hey!" Gigi said.

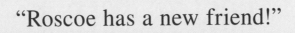

"Roscoe has a new friend!"

HOW TO FOLD A
PUPPY HEAD

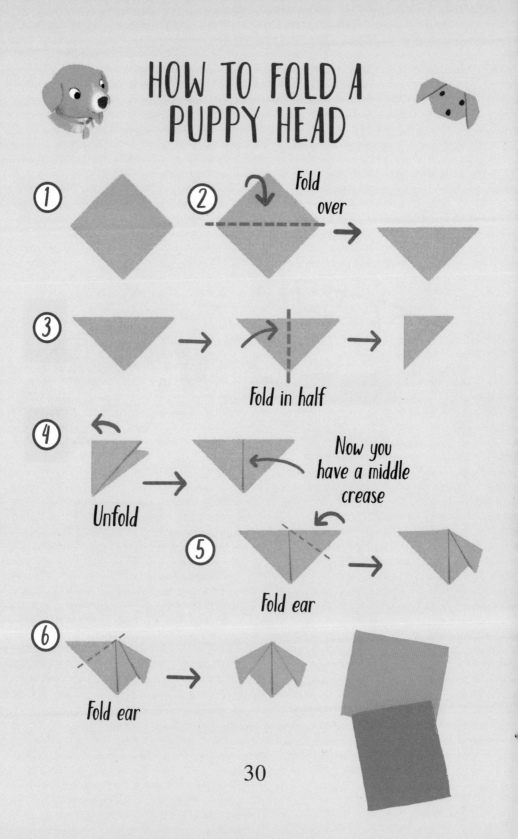

①

② Fold over

③ Fold in half

④ Unfold — Now you have a middle crease

⑤ Fold ear

⑥ Fold ear

30

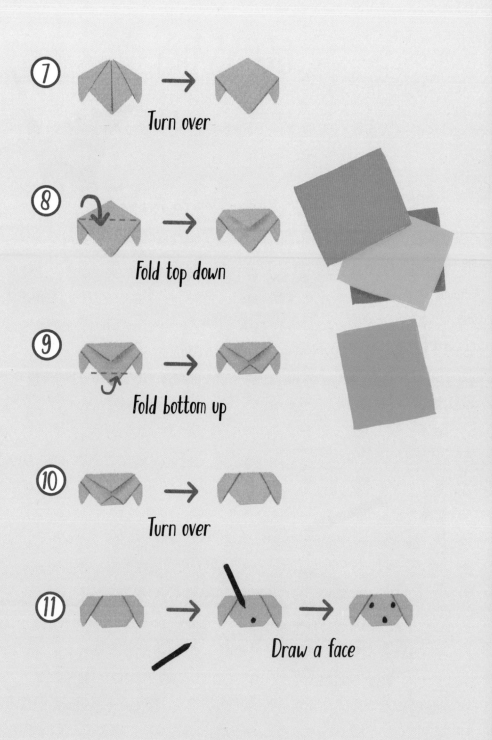

⑦ Turn over

⑧ Fold top down

⑨ Fold bottom up

⑩ Turn over

⑪ Draw a face

GLOSSARY

Ganbarimasu I will try hard, or I will do my best

Ganbatte Good luck, try hard, or do your best

Origami The Japanese art of paper folding

Ojiji A nickname for grandfather, like "grandpa"

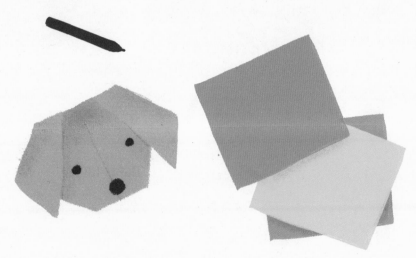